SPACE DOG and Roy

Natalie Standiford

illustrated by TONY ROSS

RED FOX

A Red Fox Book

Published by Random House Children's Books
61-63 Uxbridge Road, London, W5 5SA

A division of Random House UK Ltd
London Melbourne Sydney Auckland
Johannesburg and agencies throughout the world

5 7 9 10 8 6 4

First published by Avon Books Ltd, New York, 1990
First publised in Great Britain in 1991 by Hutchinson Children's Books

Red Fox edition 1992
This Red Fox edition 1999

Space Dog series designed and produced by
Signpost Books Ltd,
25 Eden Drive, Headington, Oxford OX3 0AB

Printed and bound in Great Britain by
Bookmarque Ltd, Croydon, Surrey

RANDOM HOUSE UK Limited Reg. No. 954009

ISBN 0 09 940092 8

www.kidsatrandomhouse.co.uk

Contents

Chapter 1

Roy Wants a Dog

It was a cold and cloudy Saturday. Roy Barnes was sitting in the house, staring out of the window. Roy was an ordinary-looking boy, with blue eyes and a friendly face. But that day his friendly face looked worried.

Roy was thinking about Stanley Moore, the school bully. Big Stan had been picking on Roy a lot lately, more than he picked on anyone else. It had got so bad that Roy didn't like going to school any more. It was all Stanley's fault.

The doorbell rang. Roy answered it. There stood Roy's friend Alice. 'Meet

Blanche, my new dog,' she said, pulling a curly black poodle round in front of her.

'Wow!' said Roy. 'Where did you get her?'

'She was my aunt's,' said Alice, leading Blanche into the house. 'My aunt moved to a building where they can't have dogs. She had to give Blanche away. And Mum said we could take her.'

'You are lucky,' said Roy. 'I wish I had a dog. If I had a big German shepherd, Stanley wouldn't pick on me any more.' He

bent down to pat Blanche. Blanche licked his fingers.

Alice straightened the little bow on Blanche's head. 'Maybe your parents will get you a dog when they see how nice Blanche is,' said Alice. 'In fact, Blanche is neater than I am.' Alice did have a way of looking a little messy.

'My parents?' said Roy. 'Get me a dog? No way.'

Suddenly they heard a loud noise. It came from upstairs. It sounded like an explosion.

'Uh-oh,' said Roy.

'What was that?' asked Alice.

The noise came again. Then a loud voice boomed, 'Why am I sneezing? Is there a DOG in this house?'

'See?' said Roy. 'Dad's allergic to dogs. Really allergic.'

'I'd better get Blanche out of here,' said Alice.

It was too late. Roy's father came downstairs. Mrs Barnes was right behind him.

Mr Barnes saw Blanche. 'Get that DOG out of the house, Alice!' yelled Mr Barnes. '*Aaaaah-CHOOOO!*'

'See you, Roy,' said Alice. She pulled the poodle out of the door as fast as she could.

When Blanche had gone, Mr Barnes started to feel better. 'For heaven's sake,

Roy,' said Mr Barnes. 'You know better than to let a dog in the house.'

'I'm sorry,' said Roy. 'I forgot.'

'Don't let it happen again, Roy,' said Mr Barnes. Then he turned to his wife. 'Love, are there any more tissues in the house?'

'I'll get them for you,' said Mrs Barnes. 'Roy, why don't you go outside and play?'

Roy looked out of the window. 'Can't,' he said. 'It's raining.'

Roy went up to his room. He sat on the bottom half of his bunk bed and took out his new library book. The book was called *How to Take Care of Your Dog.*

Chapter 2

Roy's Peculiar Feeling

That night, Roy lay awake for a long time. The skies had cleared and moonlight was shining ghostly white through the bedroom window. Roy had a strange, tingly feeling. *Something peculiar is going to happen*, he thought.

Suddenly Roy heard a noise outside. It sounded like a crash. He went to the window and looked out at the back garden.

He could see clearly in the moonlight, and there seemed to be a small heap of metal in the garden. It looked like a little mangled spaceship. Roy watched as somebody climbed out of it—dressed in a space suit.

The creature took off its helmet. Roy thought he was dreaming. The space creature looked like a dog!

'Wow!' said Roy. He pinched himself hard to make sure he wasn't asleep.

The dog was standing up like a person. It looked at the spaceship and shook its head. Then it reached into a pocket and pulled out something that looked like a map. Roy couldn't believe his eyes. At last he pulled himself away from the window and ran downstairs for a closer look.

Roy tiptoed out of the back door. Then he ran behind a bush. He could see that the dog was about his height. It had big ears and shaggy grey and white fur.

'Friend or foe?' called the dog. It seemed to know Roy was there.

Roy was scared. He didn't know what to

do. He stayed behind the bush.

The dog sat down and started tugging at his space boots. 'Hey, could you give me a hand?' it said. 'My feet are killing me.'

Roy came out from behind the bush. He walked over and helped pull off the dog's boots.

'Who are you?' Roy asked.

'I am an explorer from the planet Queekrg,' said the dog. 'I am on a scouting mission to Earth. It was supposed to be a secret mission.'

'I won't tell anybody,' said Roy.

'Thanks,' said the dog. They shook on it, hand and paw.

'Wow,' said Roy. 'Are you really from outer space? Can I call you "Space Dog"?'

'I am not a dog. I am a citizen of Queekrg, male,' said the dog. 'And I have a name already. It's Qrxztlq.'

Roy gave the dog a funny look.

'OK,' said the dog. 'Call me Space Dog.'

'My name is Roy,' said Roy. 'It's nice to meet you.'

Space Dog looked sadly at his ship. 'What a mess,' he said.

'Can you repair it?' asked Roy.

'Of course,' said the dog. 'But I will need some time.'

'Why don't you stay at *my* house while you work on it?' said Roy. 'I've always wanted a dog.'

'That is nice of you,' said Space Dog. The dog looked at the white-painted house behind Roy. It was old-fashioned, but it would do.

They had to hide the spaceship before they could go into the house.

Roy and Space Dog dragged it into the basement. They tried to be quiet so that Roy's parents wouldn't wake up.

'Oh, gosh!' Roy suddenly whispered. 'You can't live here. My father is allergic to dogs!'

'I'm not a dog,' said Space Dog, 'so your

18

father probably won't be allergic to me.'

'I just hope you're right,' said Roy. 'Anyway, we'll find out pretty fast.'

By then it was very late. Roy yawned. 'I'm sleepy.'

Space Dog yawned, too. 'Let us hit the hay,' he said.

They tiptoed upstairs to Roy's room. They went inside and closed the door.

At last Roy had a dog! He got a big basket and put a pillow in it. 'You can sleep here,' he told Space Dog.

But Space Dog had already climbed up to the top bunk of Roy's bed.

'Queekrites do not sleep in baskets,' he said. 'They sleep in beds.'

'OK,' said Roy. 'But you'll have to sleep on the bottom bunk. *I* sleep on the top.'

'All right,' said Space Dog. 'As long as it's a bed. I am whacked.'

'Me, too,' said Roy. Space Dog settled into the bottom bunk, and Roy climbed into the top.

'Good night, Roy,' said Space Dog.

'Good night, Space Dog,' said Roy. 'I'm really glad you crashed in *our* back garden.'

Chapter 3

Space Dog Joins
the Family

The next day was exciting. When Roy woke up, he heard someone snoring down below. He leaned over and saw Space Dog. It hadn't been a dream.

I really do have a dog, thought Roy.

Space Dog slept, and Roy went downstairs. He smelled sausages. His mother was in the kitchen. She was making pancakes.

'Good morning, Roy,' said Mrs Barnes.

'Good morning, Mum,' said Roy. 'Guess what?'

'What?'

Roy stopped. He didn't know what to

say next. How could he tell his mother about Space Dog?

'Roy?' said Mrs Barnes. 'What were you going to tell me?'

'Well,' said Roy. 'I, uh, found a dog. A really brilliant dog! Can I keep him?'

'A dog?' said Mrs Barnes. 'Where is he now?'

'Up in my room,' said Roy. 'He slept there last night, and he was really good. He didn't chew a single thing!'

'Oh, Roy,' said Mrs Barnes. 'You know I'd love to have a dog. But with your father's allergies . . . '

'This dog isn't like other dogs,' said Roy. 'Wait till you see him, Mum. I'll bring him downstairs.'

Roy ran to his room. Space Dog was still asleep. 'Wake up!' said Roy. 'Come and meet my mum.'

Space Dog snorted and lifted his head. 'Huh?' he grumbled. 'Where am I?'

Roy shook him. 'Come on!' he said.

Space Dog sat up. 'Whatever is cooking certainly smells good.'

'That's pancakes and sausages,' said Roy. 'But you can't eat things like that. You have to eat dog food.'

'I know a lot about Earth,' said Space Dog. 'But I do not know anything about dog food.' He stood up and added, 'Could I borrow a dressing-gown, Roy?'

'No!' said Roy. 'Dogs don't wear dressing-gowns!'

'Well, could I borrow a sweater, then?'

'Dogs don't wear any clothes at all,' said Roy.

'What do they do? Walk around naked?'

Roy looked serious. 'Listen, Space Dog,' he said. 'You *have* to behave like a dog. When you meet Mum, you have to walk on four legs, like this.' Roy got down on his hands and knees.

Space Dog laughed. 'Are you joking?' he said. 'That looks silly.'

'Trust me, Space Dog. You don't want them to know about your secret mission, do you?'

'No,' said Space Dog. 'But I don't want to look like a fool, either. Crawling on all fours, naked!'

'Space Dog, this is important,' said Roy. 'If anyone discovers you've come from outer space, that will be the end of your secret mission.'

At last Space Dog seemed to be listening.

'Scientists will come and take you away,' said Roy. 'Then they will study you, maybe even take your brain apart or something.'

Space Dog sighed. He got down and tried to walk on four legs. He was wobbly, but he did it.

They started down the stairs. 'Wag your

tail, too,' Roy whispered. 'And maybe lick Mum's hand or something.'

'That is disgusting!' said Space Dog.

At last they reached the kitchen. 'Mum,' said Roy, 'meet Space Dog!'

'Space Dog?' said Mrs Barnes. 'That's a funny name.' She patted Space Dog on the head. Space Dog tried to wag his tail. It looked like he was doing the hokey cokey.

'Is he hurt?' asked Mrs Barnes. 'He isn't wagging his tail properly.'

Just then they heard a big, loud yawn. It sounded like feeding time at the zoo.

'Uh-oh,' said Mrs Barnes. 'Your father's coming. Hide the dog, quick! Put him in the broom cupboard!'

Roy shoved Space Dog into the cupboard and closed the door.

'Hey, Roy!' Space Dog called from inside.

'What was that, Roy?' said Mrs Barnes.

'Nothing, Mum,' said Roy. 'Probably just Dad.'

Just then Mr Barnes walked into the kitchen.

'Goo-o-od morning!' he said. He took a deep breath and patted his chest. 'Ah, it's a beautiful spring day!'

Roy and his mum looked at each other. They waited for Mr Barnes to sneeze. But nothing happened.

'Do I smell sausages?' said Mr Barnes.

'Yes, love,' said Mrs Barnes. 'And pancakes. They're almost ready. Sit down and have some coffee.'

Roy and his father sat down. Mrs Barnes served breakfast. Everyone started to eat.

'Delicious,' said Mr Barnes.

Suddenly they heard someone knocking. It came from the broom cupboard. Roy and his mother looked at each other.

'What was that?' said Mr Barnes.

'I didn't hear anything,' said Mrs Barnes.

'Me, neither,' said Roy.

But they heard the knocking again.

'I think someone must be at the back door,' said Mrs Barnes.

'I think someone must be in the broom cupboard,' said Mr Barnes. 'And I'm going to find out who!' He got up and walked towards the door.

'Don't go in there, dear,' said Mrs Barnes. 'No one's in the cupboard.'

But there was more knocking.

'Someone is in the cupboard!' he said.

He opened the door wide. Space Dog bounded out.

'A DOG!' shouted Mr Barnes. 'What is a DOG doing in the broom cupboard? What about MY ALLERGIES!'

'But, Dad,' said Roy. 'You're not sneezing.'

Mr Barnes stopped shouting. He took a little sniff of air. He took a bigger sniff. Then he leaned down and put his nose in Space Dog's fur and sniffed. He still didn't sneeze. His eyes didn't water!

'Hey,' said Mr Barnes. 'Maybe I'm not allergic to this dog!'

Roy and Mrs Barnes clapped. 'Hurray!' said Roy.

'Where did he come from?' asked Mr Barnes.

'I think he's a stray,' said Roy. 'I heard him in the back garden last night. I went down and let him in. He has no collar. Can I keep him, Dad?'

'Well, I suppose so,' said Mr Barnes. 'If I don't start sneezing. Have you thought of a name?'

'Space Dog,' said Roy.

'Space Dog!' repeated Mr Barnes in amazement.

Chapter 4

Dog Training

'After breakfast we'll go and get some dog food,' Mr Barnes told Roy. 'And a lead.'

'Great, Dad,' said Roy. 'But in the meantime, could I give Space Dog some pancakes?'

'I don't think dogs like pancakes, Roy,' said Mr Barnes.

'Maybe Space Dog does,' said Roy.

'OK,' said Mr Barnes. 'Let's give it a try.'

Space Dog jumped up on to an empty chair. He waited eagerly for his breakfast.

'Oh no you don't, doggie,' said Mr Barnes. 'Down, boy.' He put a plate of pancakes on the floor.

Roy squatted down next to Space Dog. 'Sorry,' he whispered.

'Meet me in the living-room, pronto,' Space Dog whispered back. He trotted out of the kitchen without touching the pancakes.

Roy stood up. 'I'll be right back,' he told his parents. Then he left the kitchen, too.

'There's something strange about that dog,' said Mr Barnes.

'I know what you mean, love,' said Mrs Barnes. 'But Roy likes him.'

Roy went into the living room. He found Space Dog sitting on the sofa.

'What's going on here, Roy?' said Space Dog. 'Eating off the floor? Pancakes without syrup? And a man who calls me *doggie*?'

'I'm really sorry,' said Roy. 'But that's how dogs live. They don't mind being treated that way.'

'Earth dogs must be stupid,' said Space Dog.

'They're not stupid,' said Roy. 'They're just not like you.'

Space Dog sighed. 'I will have to get used to a dog's life, I suppose. But it is confusing! I learned all about Earth people for this mission. I knew they were not as advanced as Queekrites. But I did not know that I would have to behave like— like an animal!'

Roy looked unhappy. 'A dog isn't just any old animal,' he said. 'He's man's best friend! Everyone loves dogs. You'll see.'

After breakfast Roy and his father drove to the pet shop. As soon as they came back, Roy dragged Space Dog out to the back garden. He wanted to start Space Dog's training programme.

Roy brought out a collar and put it round Space Dog's neck. Space Dog pulled away. 'What do you think you're doing?' he demanded.

'The collar has our name and address on it,' said Roy. 'You need it in case you get lost.'

'I am not going to get lost,' said Space Dog. 'And if I do, I will just call you on the phone. I know all about telephones.'

'But what if somebody sees you making a call?' said Roy.

'I see your point,' said Space Dog. 'Go on.'

'This is your lead,' said Roy. 'You have to be on a lead when I take you to the park.'

'Why?'

'Well, it's a rule,' said Roy. 'All dogs have to be on leads. If your not, the park keeper could get you.'

'*Get* me?'

'He could take you to the dog's home and lock you up,' Roy explained. 'It's like jail.'

'This dog's life is getting worse and worse,' said Space Dog.

'Now,' said Roy, holding up an old tennis ball. 'Here's your ball. You can chew it if you want to.'

'No, thank you,' said Space Dog.

'I'll throw it, like this.' Roy tossed the ball across the garden. 'Now you run over, pick it up, and bring it back to me.'

Space Dog looked at Roy blankly.

'Go on,' said Roy.

Space Dog wobbled over to the ball on four legs. Then he picked it up in one paw and tossed it back to Roy.

'No, no, no!' said Roy. 'Pick it up in your mouth. You're not supposed to be able to throw!'

'But I *am* able!' Space Dog insisted.

'I know,' said Roy. 'But you have to do what I say. I'm your master.'

Space Dog looked sad. 'I thought you were my friend,' he said.

Suddenly Roy felt sorry. 'I *am* your friend,' he said. 'Forget about that master stuff. But please, will you behave like a dog?'

Roy tossed the ball again. This time, Space Dog picked it up in his mouth, trotted over to Roy, and dropped it at his feet.

'Good,' said Roy. 'You're getting the hang of it.'

Just then Roy heard a voice call, 'Hey, Roy!' It was Alice. She had Blanche with her. They came into the garden. Blanche looked beautiful, but Alice was a mess as usual. Her socks were falling down. The bow on one of her plaits was untied, and she had a dirty mark on her face.

'I'm teaching my new dog some tricks,' said Roy.

'Your new dog?' said Alice. 'But you said your father was allergic to dogs.'

'He's not allergic to *this* one,' said Roy. 'Alice, meet Space Dog.'

Space Dog was polite and stuck out his paw.

'Oh!' said Alice, shaking Space Dog's paw. 'He already knows how to shake paws! But he's rather funny-looking. What breed is he?'

'Uh, he's a mongrel,' said Roy.

Space Dog glared at Roy. A mongrel indeed!

Then Blanche walked over to Space Dog. She started sniffing his face. Space Dog wanted to say, 'Get away from me!' But he knew he couldn't—not in front of Alice.

'Look at Blanche!' said Alice. 'She likes your dog.'

'Well, I don't think Space Dog likes Blanche much,' said Roy. He shooed Blanche away from Space Dog.

Thank you, Roy, thought Space Dog. He looked at Blanche. *What a dopey face,* thought Space Dog. *I hope she won't come round here too often.*

'Go away now, Alice,' said Roy. 'Space Dog and I have work to do.'

'Blanche and I want to watch,' said

Alice. She pushed her glasses up on her nose. 'Don't we, Blanche?'

Blanche wagged her tail. Her tongue hung out. Space Dog could hardly bear looking at her.

Then Alice picked up the ball. 'Look what Blanche can do,' she said.

Alice threw the ball. Blanche ran after it. She picked it up in her mouth and took it back to Alice.

'Can Space Dog do that?' asked Alice.

'Of course he can,' said Roy. He took the ball from Alice. He tossed it across the garden. Space Dog walked after it. When he got to the ball, he stopped. The ball was all wet from Blanche's mouth.

Space Dog turned round and looked at Roy.

'Go on, Space Dog,' said Roy. 'Pick up the ball.'

Space Dog was *not* going to pick up the

ball. He stared at Roy harder.

Roy walked up to him. 'What's the matter? he whispered.

'The ball is all slobbery,' mumbled Space Dog. 'I will *not* put it in my mouth.'

'But Alice is watching!' said Roy. Roy looked back at Alice.

'Well?' said Alice.

'Well, nothing,' said Roy. 'Space Dog is just tired.'

'Of course,' said Alice. 'Well, Blanche and I have to go home now, so I can give Blanche a biscuit for being so clever.'

Off they went, Blanche wagging her tail like a real dog.

Chapter 5

Space Dog Tries Dog Food

After lunch Roy started building a kennel. He got some wood and nails from the basement. Space Dog told him what to do. The kennel was going to be Space Dog's secret workshop. Inside it he would do research about Earth.

All afternoon Roy hammered away. Space Dog wanted to help, but Roy wouldn't let him. Roy said it would look funny to see a dog building his own house.

'Besides, I don't mind,' said Roy. 'I've always wanted a kennel in the back garden.'

'When I was a young—uh—puppy,' said

Space Dog, 'I wanted a pet fish.'

'A fish?' said Roy, looking up from his work. 'Fish are boring.'

'On my planet they swim through air instead of water, so they can go anywhere. They're fun.'

'Flying fish!' said Roy. 'How great.'

'I wanted a fish very badly,' said Space Dog. 'But my mother didn't want fish scales all over the furniture.'

'Did you ever get one?' asked Roy between hammerings. 'A fish, I mean.'

'Well, I found a stray one day. I called him Zexl and took him home.'

'Oh, no,' said Roy. 'What did your mum say?'

'She took one look and said, "Get that mangy fish out of here!"' said Space Dog. 'Then Zexl whined a little, like this: "Yee yee yee". He sounded hungry. He looked at my mother with his big, sad fishy eyes.

Finally my mother said I had better feed him before I let him go.'

Roy was not hammering any more. '*Then* what happened?' he asked.

'I gave Zexl some freeze-dried qixzit powder. But he would not eat it. Mum said I was not doing it right. Then she fed him, and Zexl ate right out of her hand. Mum did not tell me to get rid of him any more. Zexl lived with us a long time.'

'That's a good story,' said Roy. 'I like the last part best.'

Roy began to hammer again.

By the end of the day the kennel was finished—except for a roof.

Roy sat back on the grass. 'A roof is hard to build,' he said. 'Maybe we can find some canvas to go over the top.'

'Yes,' said Space Dog. 'Roy, I like my new place a lot. Thank you.'

Just then, Roy's mother opened the back door. 'That's quite a kennel,' she said. And it was. It was bigger than most. It looked like a playhouse.

'Come in for supper,' said Mrs Barnes. 'We got a take-away as a surprise.'

'Let's go!' whispered Space Dog. 'I am hungry.'

'Wait a minute,' said Roy. 'You're going to have to eat dog food tonight, you know. My dad bought some for you.'

'What's it like?' asked Space Dog.

'It's a bit like stew,' said Roy. 'Just remember, you have to eat it with your mouth, not your paws.'

'Yes, yes,' said Space Dog. 'Let us go.'

They went into the house. Mrs Barnes was already at the table. Mr Barnes was opening a big, flat box. Pizza! It smelled great.

Roy sat at the table. Space Dog sat nearby on the floor. Mr Barnes said, 'Hey there, doggie. I'll get you some supper. I almost forgot about you.'

Space Dog hoped it wouldn't be dog

food after all. The dripping pizza looked delicious.

But Mr Barnes didn't cut a slice of pizza for Space Dog. He opened a tin of dog food instead. Then he plopped some brown stuff into a plastic bowl and put it on the floor.

'There you go, doggie,' he said.

Space Dog looked at the food. It didn't look very good, but he was too hungry to argue. He took a big bite.

Roy was watching when Space Dog suddenly froze. His mouth was full, but he didn't chew. Then he spat the food on to the floor and ran out of the room.

'Space Dog! Wait!' called Roy. 'It's just dog food.' He followed him out of the kitchen. But Space Dog ran upstairs to Roy's room and slammed the door.

'Hey! That dog just threw up on the floor!' said Mr Barnes angrily. 'Roy! You come back here and clean this up!'

Roy went back to the kitchen.

'Take the dog outside,' said Mr Barnes. 'He might throw up again.'

'He didn't throw up, Dad,' said Roy. 'He just doesn't like dog food.' Roy bent down to clean up the mess.

'Doesn't like dog food! Well that's just too bad,' said Mr Barnes. 'He's a dog, isn't he? So he eats dog food. I will not have a dog running this house.'

'But, Dad . . .' said Roy.

'That's final,' said Mr Barnes.

Roy ate his supper in silence. He was worried about Space Dog. There were a lot of things about being an Earth dog that seemed to make Space Dog unhappy. Roy was afraid he wouldn't have a dog very long. Space Dog might really leave.

After supper, Roy helped his father clear up. Then they turned on the dishwasher, and his father went into the living room.

Roy was alone in the kitchen at last. There were two pieces of pizza left over. He put them in a napkin and sneaked upstairs to his room. Space Dog was lying under the covers. He was reading *How to Take Care of Your Dog*.

'I'm reading the part about feeding,' he said. 'Everything in the chapter sounds awful.'

'Here,' said Roy. 'I brought you some pizza.'

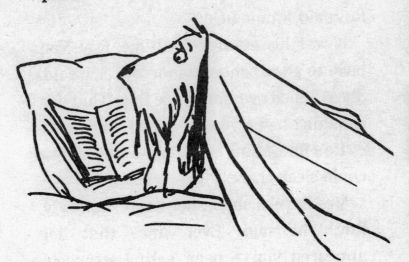

Space Dog took the napkin. He unwrapped the pizza. 'It is cold,' he said.

'I'm sorry,' said Roy. 'But I couldn't heat it up. I'm not allowed to use the oven.'

'That is OK,' said Space Dog. 'I will eat it cold.'

They sat on the bed together while Space Dog munched on the pizza. Then there was a knock at the door.

'Quick! Hide the pizza!' said Roy.

Space Dog put it under his pillow. Then Roy said, 'Come in.'

It was his mother. 'Bedtime, Roy. You have to go to school tomorrow,' she said. She reached over for Space Dog. 'That dog shouldn't be on your bed,' she said.

'He's fine, Mum,' said Roy. 'I told him he could sleep there.'

Mrs Barnes shook her head. 'Honestly, Roy,' she said. 'Ever since that dog appeared you've been acting strangely.

Now get ready for bed. I'll come back to kiss you good night.'

Space Dog pulled his pizza out from under the pillow.

'Don't let my mum see that pillowcase,' said Roy.

'Oh, sorry,' said Space Dog.

'That's OK,' said Roy. 'Maybe I can wash the pizza off tomorrow.'

Roy put on his pyjamas. Then Mr and Mrs Barnes came in and kissed him good night.

The lights were out. Space Dog's pillow smelled of cheese and tomato. He couldn't sleep.

Maybe I do not like being an Earth dog, thought Space Dog. *The food is horrible. Maybe I should start repairing my spaceship tomorrow. Then I will be able to go home. Who wants to study a dumpy old planet like Earth anyway?*

Roy was also tossing and turning.

Having a dog is great, he thought. *But it's harder than I thought it would be. Who ever heard of a dog that has to learn to be a dog? I just hope he won't hate it here. If he does, he'll leave!*

It was a hard night for both of them. At last they fell asleep.

Chapter 6

Roy Has a Bad Day

The next morning Roy's alarm clock woke Space Dog. It didn't wake Roy. Space Dog poked the bed above him. 'Hey, Roy! Wake up!'

Roy turned off the alarm, but he had trouble getting out of bed. Finally he stumbled into the bathroom. Roy didn't want to go to school. Big Stan the bully would be there waiting for him.

Space Dog went downstairs. The front door was open. He saw the newspaper on the steps outside. He went out and picked up the paper—in his mouth.

Space Dog carried the paper into the

kitchen. Mr Barnes was at the kitchen table, drinking coffee. He saw Space Dog with the newspaper.

'Good dog!' said Mr Barnes. 'You're bringing my paper!'

But Space Dog walked straight past Mr Barnes and kept on going—out of the back door to his kennel. He wanted the newspaper for his research.

'Hey!' shouted Mr Barnes. 'Bring back my paper!' He followed Space Dog outside.

Roy heard the shouting. He ran down-

stairs and out into the garden to see what was happening.

'Roy!' said Mr Barnes. 'Your dog has stolen my paper! He's in that kennel. I bet he's tearing it up.'

'I bet he's reading it,' said Roy.

'Don't joke with me, young man,' said Mr Barnes.

Roy stuck his head in the kennel. 'Space Dog, give Dad his paper,' he said. 'You can have it after he's read it.'

Space Dog handed Roy the paper. Roy handed it to his father.

'Thank you,' said Mr Barnes. He marched back into the house.

'I have to go in to breakfast,' Roy told Space Dog.

'What about me?' said Space Dog.

'I'll bring you some toast before I go to school. Bye.'

'Bye, Roy,' said Space Dog.

Roy got to school without running into bully Stan. That was good. He sat down at his desk and then remembered that maths was his first class. Roy was no good at maths.

'Hi, Roy,' said Alice. She had the desk next to Roy's. 'How's your new dog?'

'He's fine,' said Roy. 'I just hope he's happy.'

'Why shouldn't he be?' said Alice. 'It doesn't take much to make a dog happy.'

'That's what you think,' said Roy.

Ms Humphrey came in and told everyone to open their workbook on page thirty-nine. She told the class to do the problems on that page.

Roy tried to multiply, but he couldn't keep his mind on maths. He was thinking about Space Dog. Would he remember to behave like a dog when Roy's mother was around? Would his mother force Space

Dog to eat dog food?

'Roy? Roy?' said Ms Humphrey. 'I want the answer to the first problem.'

Roy sat up. 'Um, the answer is seven,' he said.

'Wrong, Roy,' said Ms Humphrey. 'You had better pay attention. We are having a test on this tomorrow.'

Oh, help, thought Roy. *This is turning into a bad day.*

At break time, Roy and Alice climbed on the monkey bars. Alice hung upside-down. Roy held her glasses.

'Maybe Blanche and Space Dog will fall in love,' said Alice. 'Wouldn't that be great?'

'No, it wouldn't,' said Roy. Alice was still upside-down. Roy reached over for her plaits. He tried to tie them in a knot.

'Stop it!' said Alice. 'Blanche and Space Dog could get married and have puppies. Then we would be related!'

'What a stupid idea,' said Roy. 'Dogs don't get married.'

'At least they could play together while we are at school. I think Blanche gets lonely.'

'Space Dog won't get lonely,' said Roy. 'He has things to do.'

'What things?' said Alice, still in her upside-down position.

'Oh. Uh, things like digging holes in the back garden,' said Roy.

Alice swung down from the monkey bars. Her face was all red and hot from being upside-down. She walked over to the water fountain. Roy started to follow her, but all of a sudden he tripped and fell flat on his face.

'Ha, ha, ha!' laughed a big fat voice. It was big fat Stanley. He had tripped Roy on purpose.

'You leave him alone!' said Alice. She pushed up her glasses.

'How are you going to make me, Four Eyes?' said Stanley.

'I'll set my dog on you,' said Alice.

'Oh! I'm scared, I'm scared!' said Stanley in a high, squeaky voice. 'Your prissy little poodle is going to hurt me.'

The bell rang. Roy brushed himself down. 'Let's go, Alice,' he said. They started to walk back into the school building.

'Look out this afternoon, Barnes!' Stanley called after Roy. 'You might run into me on your way home from school.'

'What a twit,' said Alice. 'Don't worry, Roy. He's all bark and no bite.'

'I know,' said Roy, but he wasn't too sure at all.

Chapter 7

Roy Is Scared

Roy was nervous all the way home from school. He was waiting for Stanley to strike. He glanced behind bushes and parked cars, but he didn't see the bully.

This is crazy, thought Roy. *I have to do something. Maybe Space Dog can help. After all, he is a dog. Sort of.*

When Roy got home, he went straight to the back garden. Space Dog was in his kennel. He was working on something that looked like an engine.

'Hi, Roy,' said Space Dog. 'How was school?'

'Not great,' said Roy. 'I have a problem.'

Space Dog put down his screwdriver. He offered Roy some custard creams. He had taken them from the kitchen when Mrs Barnes wasn't looking.

'What kind of problem?' asked Space Dog. 'Maths? I love maths problems.'

'It isn't a maths problem,' said Roy. 'It's a bully problem. This boy called Stanley hates me. He says he's going to beat me up. He's very big, Space Dog.'

'I know about bullies,' said Space Dog. 'On Queekrg I worked with a scientist named Tzaxette. She was big. She was mean. Every time I had a good idea, she punched me.'

'What did you do?' asked Roy.

'I offered to go on this mission,' said Space Dog. 'It meant I could get away from her.'

'That won't work for me,' said Roy. 'School is my problem. But I have to go. I

was thinking maybe you could help me.'

'Me?' said Space Dog. 'What can I do?'

'A lot of people are afraid of dogs,' said Roy. 'Maybe you could scare Stanley.'

'How? If he is bigger than you, he is bigger than I am. He could beat me up.'

'Not if you act fierce,' said Roy. 'Try it. Show your teeth. Growl.'

'Growl?' said Space Dog.

'Like this,' said Roy. '*Grr*. Now you try it.'

Space Dog stuck out his lips and said: 'Gerbil.'

'Try again,' said Roy. '*Grrr!*'

'Gurgle.'

'No, no,' said Roy. '*Grrr* isn't a word. It's a sound. Maybe Blanche should teach you.'

'Not Blanche!' said Space Dog. 'I do not want her near me.'

'Try it once more,' said Roy. '*Grrrrr!*'

'Gir-r-r-r-dle!'

gerbil

'I give up,' said Roy. 'No one's going to be scared of a dog who growls "girdle".'

'Sorry,' said Space Dog.

Roy munched on a biscuit for a minute, thinking. Then he said, 'Maybe you don't need to growl. Maybe if Stanley just *sees* you, he'll be scared. Will you come to school with me tomorrow?'

'Great!' said Space Dog. 'I would love to see an Earth school at first hand. Will I be able to sit next to you?'

'No,' said Roy. 'You can't go into the building. We'll just walk to and from school together. In between you'll have to be tied up in the playground.'

'So dogs cannot go to school,' said Space Dog. 'No wonder Blanche seems so dumb.'

'Will you do it?' asked Roy. 'Will you walk to school with me?'

'No way,' said Space Dog. 'How would *you* like to be tied up all day?'

'I'd hate it,' said Roy. 'Oh well, I'll just have to think of something else.'

Space Dog knew he had let Roy down. He tried to make up for it. 'Do you need any help with your homework?' he asked. 'I would be good at that.'

Roy smiled. 'No, thanks,' he said. Space Dog started working on the engine again.

'What's that?' asked Roy.

'The main engine from my spaceship. I am trying to repair it,' said Space Dog.

'Oh,' said Roy. 'Well, I should go and tell Mum I'm home. See you later.'

Roy went into the house. Then it hit him. Space Dog was working on his engine. That meant he *was* going to leave!

Chapter 8

Space Dog to the Rescue

The next morning Roy woke up with butterflies in his stomach. *Last week I only had one thing to worry about,* he thought. *That was Stanley. This week I have two things to worry about—Stanley and Space Dog. I have to get Space Dog to stay. I just have to!*

Space Dog was still asleep. Roy listened to him snore. *He's cute when he snores,* Roy thought sadly.

Then the butterflies came back again. *Ugh, I have to go to school today,* he thought. *I wish Stanley would go to live somewhere different. Like Egypt.*

Roy forced himself to get dressed. Then he went downstairs to the kitchen. He drank some orange juice, but he didn't eat anything. He started off to school with a heavy heart.

Space Dog worked on his engine most of the day. It was a big job. He needed more time.

In the afternoon he took a break and began reading Mr Barnes's newspaper. He turned to the cartoons. Suddenly he felt as if someone was watching him.

Space Dog looked up. Blanche was standing in the door of the kennel. She was panting.

'Oh, no,' said Space Dog. 'Not you again.'

Blanche started nosing her way further into the kennel.

'Go away!' said Space Dog. 'I am busy.'

Blanche whined. She stuck her wet nose closer. She tried to lick his ear.

'Scat!' said Space Dog. 'This place is top secret!' He pushed Blanche out of the kennel, but she came straight back in. Then he walked out of the kennel. Blanche followed him. He started to run. Blanche trotted along behind.

'Help!' shouted Space Dog. He ran out of the garden. Blanche was hard on his heels. He jumped over a hedge for the first time in his life. Blanche jumped the hedge easily.

Down the pavement they ran, Space Dog barely in the lead. They raced across drives and even a street. Cars honked their horns and put on their brakes.

'I am sorry!' cried Space Dog. No one

heard him because he was running too fast. And Blanche was still right behind.

Space Dog didn't know it, but he was running towards Roy's school. School was just finishing.

Roy was walking home from school. He noticed one of his trainers was untied. He knelt down to tie it. *That's all I need*, he thought. *I'll trip over my own shoelace just as I'm running away from Stan.*

Just then Stanley came up behind Roy. 'Hello, Roy-Boy,' he teased. 'Shoe trouble? Let me help you.' Stanley leaned over and pulled off Roy's trainer.

'Hey! Give that back!' shouted Roy. He hopped after Stanley on one foot.

Stanley was a lot taller than Roy. He dangled the trainer over Roy's head. 'Come and get it,' he said. 'It's right here.'

Roy hopped and jumped. The shoe

stayed just out of reach. Stanley thought it was very funny.

Roy was about to cry. He tried to sound tough. 'You'd better give me that shoe,' he said. His voice sounded a little squeaky. 'Or I'll . . . I'll set my dog on you!'

Stanley just laughed. 'You don't even have a dog,' he said. 'If you did, he'd be a little pipsqueak like you.'

Just then Roy saw Space Dog running down the pavement towards him. *Just in time!* thought Roy. *Come on, Space Dog!*

Space Dog saw Roy at exactly the same moment. *Just in time!* thought Space Dog. *Save me, Roy!*

Space Dog ran up and hid behind Roy. When Blanche saw Roy, she came skidding to a stop.

'Go away, Blanche,' said Roy. 'Go home!' Roy knew Space Dog didn't like Alice's poodle.

Poor Blanche. She didn't want to leave Space Dog. At last she turned round and set off home. This time her tail wasn't wagging.

Stanley looked at Space Dog. Space Dog was tired and out of breath. He was still hiding behind Roy's legs. 'Is that your dog?' said Stanley. 'He *is* a pipsqueak! I knew it!'

'Stanley, give me my trainer,' said Roy.

So this is Stanley, thought Space Dog. He looked at the nasty face. He looked at Roy's shoe. All of a sudden, he understood. Stanley was bullying Roy again. He knew what he had to do.

Space Dog tried to growl. '*Garur, garur,*' he said. He walked towards Stanley and growled louder. '*Garur, garur.*' Stanley didn't drop the shoe.

'Your little dog doesn't scare me,' he said.

Space Dog growled again. '*Grrrr!*' Then he nipped Big Stanley on the ankle.

'Ouch!' cried Stanley. He dropped Roy's shoe and held his leg. 'Keep that dog away from me! He's probably got rabies!' Stanley limped away as fast as he could.

Space Dog spat out some wool from Stanley's sock. 'Well,' he said. 'Was I OK?'

'Oh, Space Dog!' said Roy, hugging him. 'You saved me! You're the best friend I ever had!'

'Aw, it was nothing,' said Space Dog. 'And anyway, I owed you a favour. You saved me from Blanche.'

Roy hugged Space Dog tighter. Space Dog didn't say anything, but he liked it. No one hugged on Queekrg, but maybe he could learn how.

Chapter 9

Howling in the Back Garden

For dinner that night, the Barneses had meatloaf. It was not Roy's favourite. It was not Space Dog's favourite, either. It reminded him of dog food.

'Mum and Dad,' said Roy. 'From now on I will feed Space Dog. I'm big enough to take care of him myself.'

Mr Barnes patted Roy on the back. 'That's what I like to hear, Roy!' he said. 'You're growing up.'

Mrs Barnes smiled proudly.

Space Dog smiled, too. He knew what this meant. After every meal, Roy could feed him *real* food. No more dog food!

And that was exactly what happened. After dinner, Roy put meatloaf with some tomato ketchup on a paper plate. Space Dog ate it in Roy's room, with a knife and a fork and a napkin on his lap.

'Meatloaf isn't so bad,' he said. 'It looks like dog food, but it's ten times tastier.'

'Are you ready for a surprise?' said Roy. 'Here's your pudding.' Roy uncovered a little bowl of orange jelly with whipped cream.

'Orange jelly!' cried Space Dog. 'My favourite! Thank you, Roy.'

'You're welcome.'

Space Dog tucked into the jelly. Suddenly he and Roy heard a strange sound. It came from the back garden. 'AaaOOO! AaaOOOOO!'

Roy and Space Dog looked at each other. 'What's that?' asked Roy.

Space Dog shrugged. He went to the window.

'AaaOOOOOO!'

Space Dog and Roy looked out and saw Blanche in the garden. She was staring at Roy's bedroom window, howling. It sounded like love howls.

Roy smiled and looked up at the night sky. The moon was bright again. He remembered life before Space Dog. He had wanted a dog so much. *Now everything is different*, he thought. *I have a*

dog. *More than a dog. Better than a dog. I have a best friend. If only he would stay!*

Space Dog was looking at the moon, too. He thought about his planet and his friends there. *I never had a better friend than Roy*, he thought. *No one ever tried harder to make me happy.*

The two stood quietly side by side, thinking. Finally Roy broke the silence. He could not stand the suspense any longer.

'How's your engine coming along?' he asked.

'It's not repaired yet,' said Space Dog. 'But I think I will stop working on it for now. I will not need it for some time.'

'Does that mean you're not going to leave?'

'Leave?' said Space Dog. 'And go back to Tzaxette?'

Roy laughed.

'She's worse than Stanley,' said Space Dog.

Roy and Spac[...]
Outside Blanche ho[...]
friends fell happily asleep,[...]
over their heads.